Thank You

How to turn a grey day into a Yay day!

written and illustrated by Josh Langley

First published 2024

Big Sky Publishing Pty Ltd
PO Box 303, Newport, NSW 2106, Australia
Phone: 1300 364 611
Fax: (61 2) 9918 2396
Email: info@bigskypublishing.com.au
Web: www.bigskypublishing.com.au
Cover design and typesetting: Think Productions
National Library of Australia Cataloguing-in-Publication entry (pbk.)
Author: Josh Langley
Title: Thank You! How to turn a grey day into a Yay day
ISBN: 978-1-923144-12-5

Thank You

How to turn a grey day into a Yay day!

written and illustrated by Josh Langley

For Kali.

I'm so grateful you're part of our little family.

Growing up, I didn't like that I was short, wore glasses, couldn't spell, and had trouble staying focused.

Now that I'm an adult, I haven't changed – I'm still short, I still wear glasses, I still can't spell or concentrate!

But one thing has changed.

It's the way I think about myself.

All those things that made me feel different, in fact made me who I am. And now I can say that I'm grateful for all those things because without them, I wouldn't be me.

I am enough the way I am, and so are you.

And for that I'm truly grateful.

– Josh

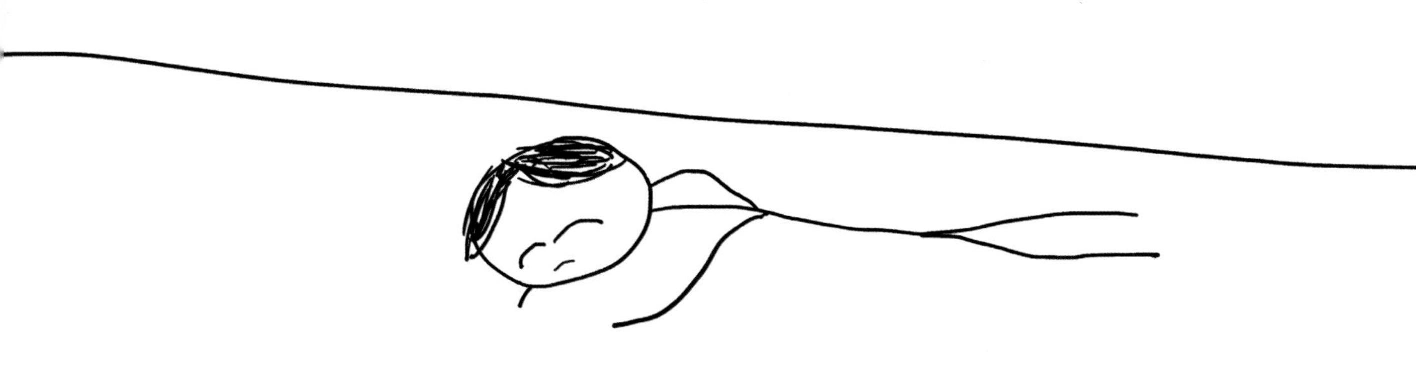

Most days are pretty awesome, but some days can feel a bit BLAH.

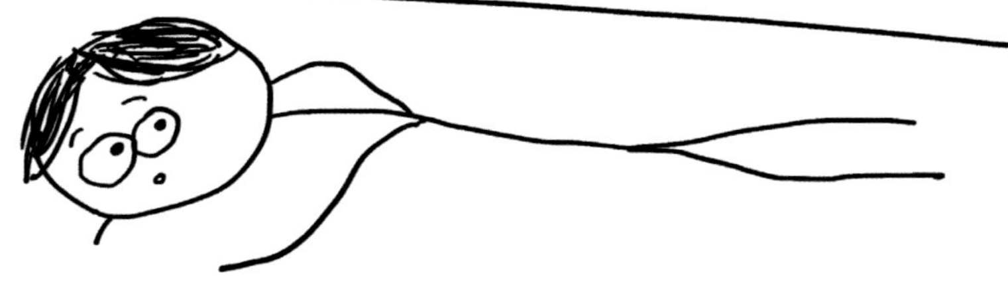

However, you can turn those BLAH days into YAY days.

And it's pretty easy to do.

Ready to find out how?

Discover the power

behind a thank you.

That special power is called GRATITUDE.

Gratitude is when you think about something, and it makes you feel wonderful on the inside.

Like a buzzy happy feeling.

Like your heart is super-charged.

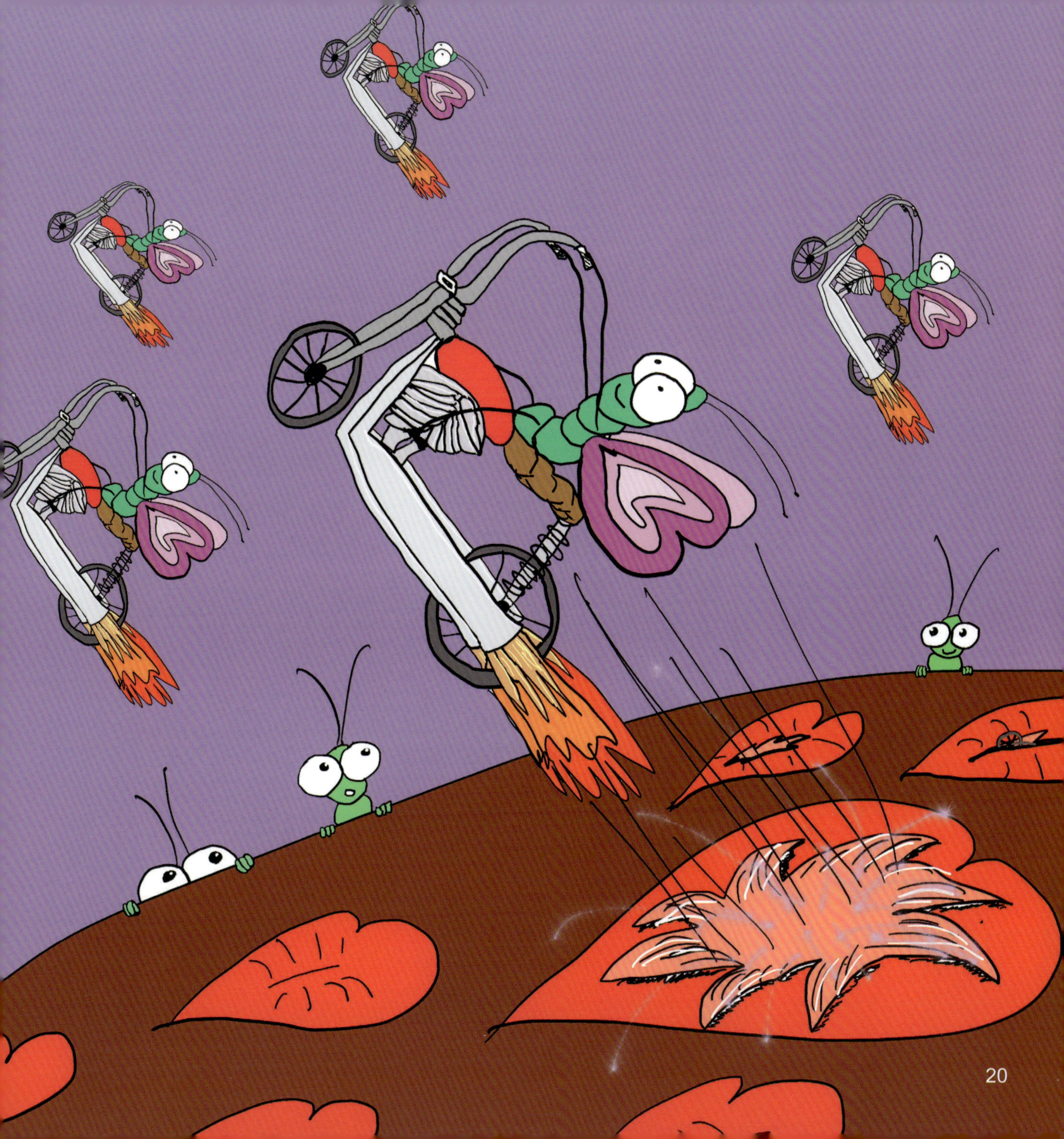

It starts with a positive
thought in your mind.

Soon that thought can become
a joyful feeling inside you.

That's how you turn a grey day...

...into a YAY day!

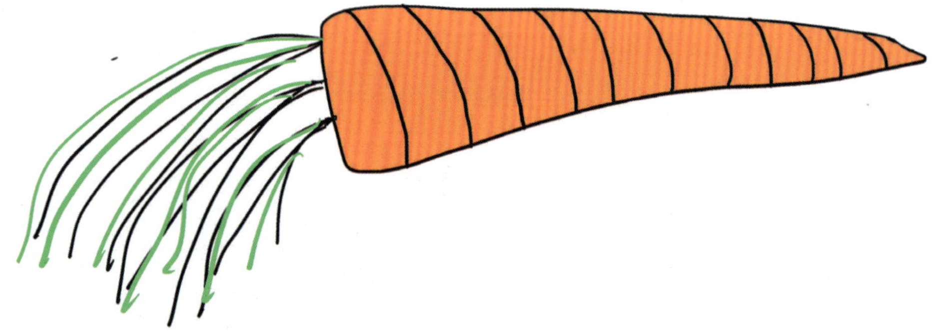

How

gratitude works

Think about something you're grateful for.

You could be grateful for anything!

Spaghetti, a pet guinea pig, having someone who loves you, clean water, kitty cats, gaming, flowers, music or snails!

Then notice how it feels in your body when you think about it.

When you feel gratitude for something,
it should feel awesome!

It could be a happy feeling.

A buzzy feeling.

A joyful feeling.

Or you could feel all warm on the inside.

That's the feeling of gratitude.

Living with a

grateful heart

When you feel gratitude for what you have in your life, the world feels so much better!

You feel happier.

Friends are nicer.

You feel like doing more things.

And more good things seem to happen.

But more importantly, you have the power to change how you feel with only a thought!

If you're feeling down, sad or flat...

Sit quietly and think of something you're grateful for (something that makes you feel good on the inside), and you'll start to feel better.

A big thank you

from your heart

When you are grateful for something
you can say a big 'thank you' to whatever
that something or somebody might be.

THANK YOU!

Thank you for trees.

Thank you for rainbows.

Thank you for flowers.

Thank you for dinosaurs.
Thank you for toilet paper.

Thank you for pet fish.

Thank you for cheese.

Thank you for butterflies.
And thank you for books.

It's Ok to Feel the Way You Do
It's OK to feel the way you do
otherwise you wouldn't be you!
written and illustrated by Josh Langley

The magic of

a thank you

What could be even more amazing about feeling gratitude and saying thank you to someone?

Not only can you change how you feel but you can change how other people feel too.

When you say thank you, and really mean it, you send your good energy to the other person.

So, you both get to share in that great feeling.

Don't hold back.

Find ways to say 'thank you' every day and you'll turn those BLAH days into YAY days!

THANK YOU!

To make it easy, write a big list of things you're grateful for.

Call it your 'thank you' list.

Then pick your top 10.

Stick it on your bedroom wall, or on the fridge, so you can read it every day.

THANK YOU LIST
1. SNAILS
2. TOILETS
3. ANDY
4. LOVE.
5. RAINBOWS
6. DOGS
7. PASTA

One last thing ...

Thank you for being amazing.

Thank you for being who you are in all your wonderfulness.

Thank you for being you.

You make everyday a Yay day too.

Things I'm grateful for ...

More things I'm grateful for ...

Even more things I'm grateful for!

And here's a few more!

THANK
YOU!
WITH
JOSH

Thank you to the team at Big Sky Publishing
for being awesome once again:
Diane, Sharon, Allison, Jodee and Denny.

Thank you to Andy for believing in me.

Thank you to you for reading this book.

Helping kids make friends with themselves

Download Josh's FREE mini ebook "9 Super Skills for kid's better mental health".

These 9 Super Skills are widely known to have a powerful effect on kids emotional and mental wellbeing now and well into the future, and can help reduce the risk of anxiety and depression.

So, what are these skills and what difference will they make?

Let's find out.

Other books in the
Being You is Enough series

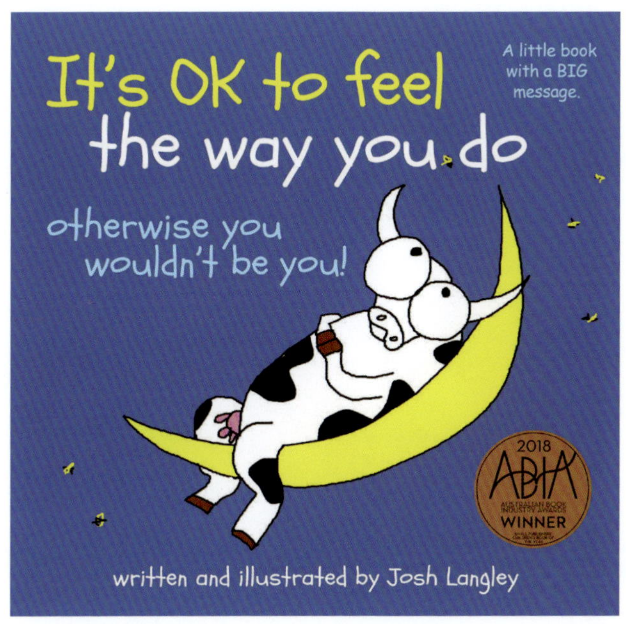

Everyone has feelings ...
sometimes we just don't know what to do with them!

Happy, sad, lonely, angry, anxious, proud, scared – they're all feelings and emotions and they're all OK! Yes – every single one of them!

In this bright and heartening book Josh Langley helps kids get to know and make friends with their feelings.

It's Ok to Feel the Way You Do empowers kids to understand and share their feelings so they can enjoy life a whole lot more.

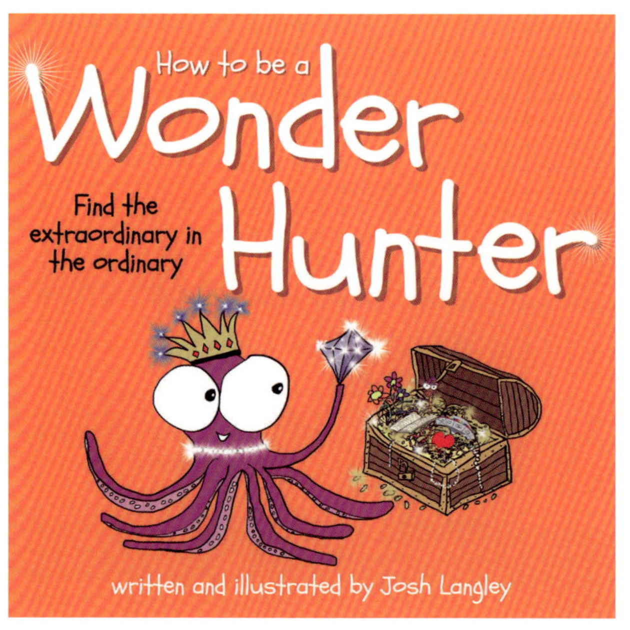

How to be a Wonder Hunter invites kids to put down their devices and go on exciting new adventures and find out how to turn the ordinary into the extraordinary!

Set out like a field guide, this entertaining and refreshing book shows children how to use their senses, imagination and natural curiosity to learn how to deeply interact with the world around them and the world inside them.

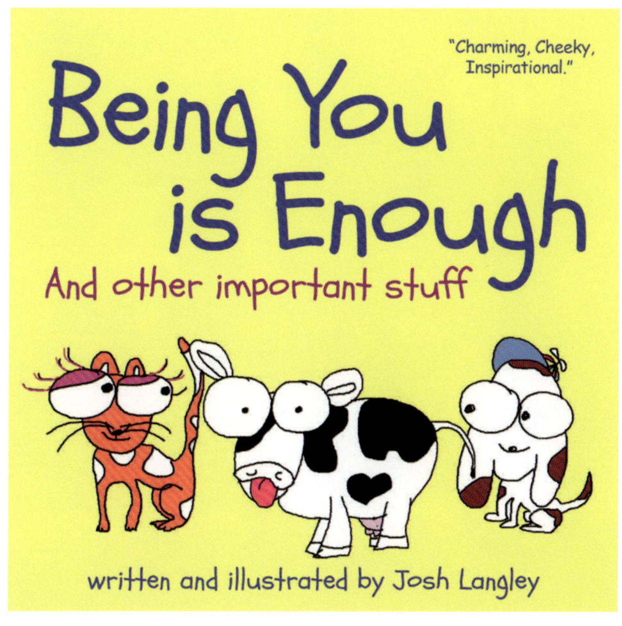

Being You Is Enough is the perfect antidote for the pressures of being a kid in this day and age. This entertaining and refreshing book will inspire kids be themselves and stand up tall.

Kids will love the easy, upbeat style delivering deeper messages about self-acceptance, positive thinking and friendship.

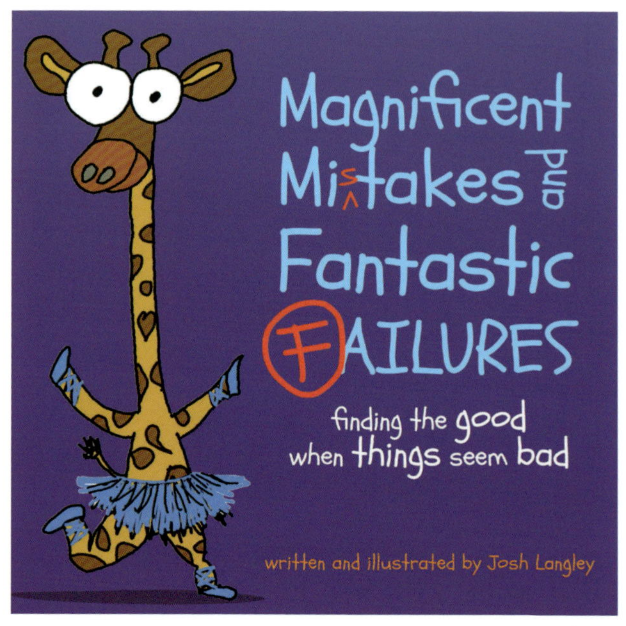

Mistakes can be magnificent! Failures can be fantastic!
And problems can be turned upside down!

Refreshingly simple and delightfully quirky, *Magnificent Mistakes and Fantastic Failures*, will help kids build resilience.

They'll discover how life's little upsets can be big opportunities to learn and grow.

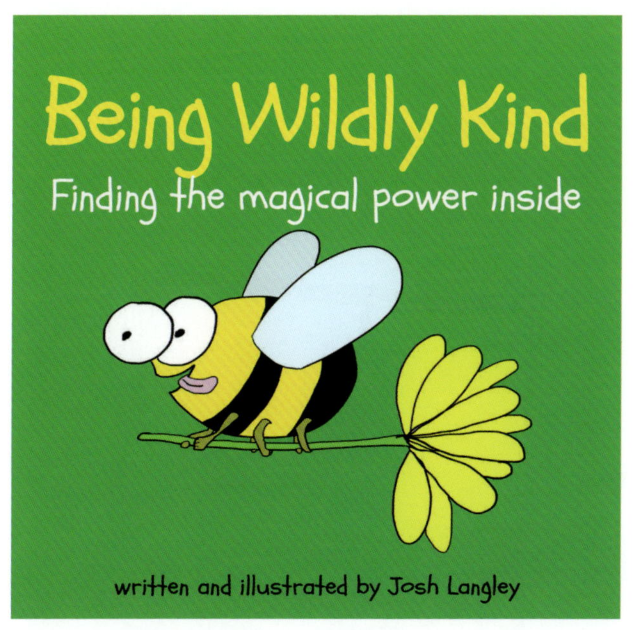

Being Wildly Kind is an infectious, fun and hope-filled book packed full of ideas to build empathy and compassion in kids of all ages.

Why just be kind when you can be WILDLY KIND?
Be WILDLY KIND to people! Be WILDLY KIND to animals!
Be WILDLY KIND to the planet! Being WILDLY KIND is a magical power that can help change the world in big and small ways.

You can now watch Josh talk about the themes of his books with the *Inspiring Kids* video series.

www.joshlangley.com.au